RUSKIN BOND

GREAT STORIES
FOR CHILDREN
Volume 3

MOONSTONE

Published in Moonstone
by Rupa Publications India Pvt. Ltd 2023
7/16, Ansari Road, Daryaganj
New Delhi 110002

Sales centres:
Prayagraj Bengaluru Chennai
Hyderabad Jaipur Kathmandu
Kolkata Mumbai

P-ISBN: 978-93-5702-440-2
E-ISBN: 978-93-5702-430-3

First impression 2023

10 9 8 7 6 5 4 3 2 1

The Overcoat

It was clear frosty weather, and as the moon rose over the Himalayan peaks, I could see patches of snow still lay on the roads of the hill-station. I would have been quite happy in bed, with a book and a hot-water bottle at my side, but I'd promised the Kapadias that I'd go to their party, and I felt it would be churlish of me to stay away. I put on two sweaters, an old football scarf, and an overcoat, and set off down the moonlit road.

It was a walk of just over a mile to the Kapadias' house, and I had covered about half the distance when I saw a girl standing in the middle of the road.

She must have been sixteen or seventeen. She looked rather old-fashioned – long hair, hanging to her waist, and a flummoxy sequined dress, pink and lavender, that reminded me of the photos in my grandmother's family album. When I went closer, I noticed that she had lovely eyes and a winning smile.

'Good evening,' I said. 'It's a cold night to be out.'

'Are you going to the party?' she asked.

'That's right. And I can see from your lovely dress that you're going too. Come along, we're nearly there.'

She fell into step beside me and we soon saw lights from the Kapadias' house shining brightly through the deodars. The girl told me her name was Julie. I hadn't seen her before, but I'd only been in the hill-station a few months.

There was quite a crowd at the party, and no one seemed to know Julie. Everyone thought she was a friend of mine. I did not deny it. Obviously she was someone who was feeling lonely and wanted to be friendly with people. And she was certainly enjoying herself. I did not see her do much eating or drinking, but she flitted about from one group to another, talking, listening, laughing; and when the music began, she was dancing almost continuously, alone or with partners, it didn't matter which, she was completely wrapped up in the music.

It was almost midnight when I got up to go. I had drunk a fair amount of punch, and I was ready for bed. As I was saying goodnight to my hosts and wishing everyone a Merry Christmas, Julie slipped her arm into mine and said she'd be going home too.

When we were outside, I said, 'Where do you live, Julie?'

'At Wolfsburn,' she said. 'Right at the top of the hill.'

'There's a cold wind,' I said. 'And although your dress is beautiful, it doesn't look very warm. Here, you'd better wear my overcoat. I've plenty of protection.'

She did not protest, and allowed me to slip my overcoat over her shoulders. Then we started out on the walk home.

But I did not have to escort her all the way. At about the spot where we had met, she said, 'There's a short cut from here. I'll just scramble up the hillside.'

'Do you know it well?' I asked. 'It's a very narrow path.'

'Oh, I know every stone on the path. I use it all the time. And besides, it's a really bright night.'

'Well, keep the coat on,' I said. 'I can collect it tomorrow.'

She hesitated for a moment, then smiled and nodded. She then disappeared up the hill, and I went home alone.

The next day I walked up to Wolfsburn. I crossed a little brook, from which the house had probably got its name, and entered an open iron gate. But of the house itself, little remained. Just a roofless ruin, a pile of stones, a shattered chimney, a few Doric pillars where a veranda had once stood.

Had Julie played a joke on me? Or had I found the wrong house?

I walked around the hill, to the mission house where the Taylors lived and asked old Mrs Taylor if she knew a girl called Julie.

'No, I don't think so,' she said. 'Where does she live?'

'At Wolfsburn, I was told. But the house is just a ruin.'

'Nobody has lived at Wolfsburn for over forty years. The Mackinnons lived there.

One of the old families that settled here. But when their girl died…' She stopped and gave me a queer look. 'I think her name was Julie…Anyway, when she died, they sold the house and went away. No one ever lived in it again, and it fell into decay. But it couldn't be the same Julie you're looking for. She died of consumption – there wasn't much you could do about it in those days. Her grave is in the cemetery, just down the road.'

I thanked Mrs Taylor and walked slowly down the road to the cemetery; not really wanting to know any more, but propelled forward almost against my will.

It was a small cemetery under the deodars. You could see the eternal snows of the Himalayas standing out against the pristine blue of the sky. Here lay the bones of forgotten empire-builders – soldiers, merchants, adventurers, their wives and children. It did not take me long to find Julie's grave. It had a simple headstone with her name clearly outlined on it:

Julie Mackinnon

1923-39

'With us one moment,

Taken the next,

Gone to her Maker,

Gone to her rest.'

Julie Mackinnon
1923-39
'With us one moment,
Taken the next,
Gone to her Maker,
Gone to her rest.'

Although many monsoons had swept across the cemetery wearing down the stones, they had not touched this little tombstone.

I was turning to leave when I caught a glimpse of something familiar behind the headstone. I walked round to where it lay.

Neatly folded on the grass was my overcoat.

No thank-you note. But something soft and invisible brushed against my cheek, and I knew someone was trying to thank me.

Wild Fruit

It was a long walk to school. Down the hill, through the rhododendron trees, across a small stream, around a bare, brown hill, and then through the narrow little bazaar, past fruit stalls piled high with oranges, guavas, bananas, and apples.

The boy's gaze often lingered on those heaps of golden oranges – oranges grown in the plains, now challenging the pale winter sunshine in the hills. His nose twitched

at the sharp smell of melons in summer; his fingers would sometimes touch for a moment the soft down on the skin of a peach. But these were forbidden fruit. The boy hadn't the money for them.

He took one meal at seven in the morning when he left home; another at seven in the evening when he returned from school. There were times – especially when he was at school, and his teacher droned on and on, lecturing on honesty, courage, duty, and self-sacrifice – when he felt very hungry; but on the way to school, or on the way home, there was nearly always the prospect of some wild fruit.

The boy's name was Vijay, and he belonged to a village near Mussoorie. His parents tilled a few narrow terraces on the hill slopes. They grew potatoes, onions, barley, maize; barely enough to feed themselves. When greens were scarce, they boiled the tops of the stinging-nettle and made them into a dish resembling spinach.

Vijay's parents realised the importance of sending him to school, and it didn't cost them much, except for the books. But it was all of four miles to the town, and a long walk makes a boy hungry.

But there was nearly always the wild fruit.

The purple berries of the thorny bilberry bushes, ripening in May and June. Wild strawberries, growing in shady places like spots of blood on the deep green monsoon grass. Small, sour cherries, and tough medlars. Vijay's strong teeth and probing tongue extracted whatever tang or sweetness lay hidden in them. And in March there were the rhododendron flowers.

His mother made them into jam. But Vijay liked them as they were. He placed the petals on his tongue and chewed them till the sweet juice trickled down his throat. But in November, there was no wild fruit. Only acorns on the oak trees, and they were bitter, fit only for the monkeys.

He walked confidently through the bazaar, strong in his legs. He looked like a healthy boy, until you came up close and saw the patches on his skin and the dullness in his eyes.

He passed the fruit stalls, wondering who ate all that fruit, and what happened to the fruit that went bad; he passed the sweet shop, where hot, newly-fried jalebis lay protected like twisted orange jewels in a glass case, and where a fat, oily man raised a knife and plunged it deep into a thick slab of rich amber-coloured halwa.

The saliva built up in Vijay's mouth; there was a dull ache in his stomach. But his eyes gave away nothing of the sharp pangs he felt.

And now, a confectioner's shop. Glass jars filled with chocolates, peppermints, toffees – sweets he didn't know the names of, English sweets – wrapped up in bits of coloured paper.

A boy had just bought a bag of sweets. He had one in his mouth. He was a well-dressed boy; coins jingled in his pocket. The sweet moved from one cheek to the other. He bit deep into it, and Vijay heard the crunch and looked up. The boy smiled at Vijay, but moved away.

They met again, further along the road. Once again the boy smiled, even looked as though he was about to offer Vijay a sweet; but this time, Vijay shyly looked away. He did not want it to appear that he had noticed the sweets, or that he hungered for one.

But he kept meeting the boy, who always managed to reappear at some corner, sucking a sweet, moving it about in his mouth, letting it show between his wet lips – a sticky green thing, temptingly, lusciously beautiful.

The bag of sweets was nearly empty.

Reluctantly, Vijay decided to overtake the boy, forget

all about the sweets, and hurry home. Otherwise, he would be tempted to grab the bag and run!

And then, he saw the boy leave the bag on a bench, look at him once, and smile – smile shyly and invitingly – before moving away.

Was the bag empty? Vijay wondered with mounting excitement. It couldn't be, or it would have blown away almost immediately. Obviously, there were still a few sweets in it.

The boy had disappeared. He had gone for his tea, and Vijay could have the rest of the sweets.

Vijay took the bag and jammed it into a pocket of his shirt. Then he hurried homewards. It was getting late, and he wanted to be home before dark.

As soon as he was out of town, he opened the bag and shook the sweets out. Their red wrappers glowed like rubies in the palm of his hand.

Carefully, he undid a wrapper. There was no sweet inside, only a smooth, round stone.

Vijay found stones in all the wrappers. In his mind's eye, Vijay saw the smiling face of the boy in the bazaar: a boy who smiled sweetly but exchanged stones for sweets.

Forcing back angry tears, Vijay flung the stones down the hillside. Then he shouldered his bag of books and began the long walk home.

There were patches of snow on the ground. The grass was a dirty brown, the bushes were bare.

There is no wild fruit in November.

The Night the Roof Blew Off

We are used to sudden storms, up here on the first range of the Himalayas. The old building in which we live has, for more than a hundred years, received the full force of the wind as it sweeps across the hills from the east.

We'd lived in the building for more than ten years without a disaster. It had even taken the shock of a severe earthquake. As my granddaughter Dolly said, 'It's difficult to tell the new cracks from the old!'

It's a two-storey building, and I live on the upper floor with my family: my three grandchildren and their parents. The roof is made of corrugated tin sheets, the ceiling of wooden boards. That's the traditional Mussoorie roof.

Looking back at the experience, it was the sort of thing that should have happened in a James Thurber's story, like the dam that burst or the ghost who got in. But I wasn't thinking of Thurber at the time, although a few of his books were among the many I was trying to save from the icy rain pouring into my bedroom.

Our roof had held fast in many a storm, but the wind that night was really fierce. It came rushing at us with a high-pitched, eerie wail. The old roof groaned and protested. It took a battering for several hours while the rain lashed against the windows and the lights kept coming and going.

There was no question of sleeping, but we remained in bed for warmth and comfort. The fire had long since gone out, as the chimney had collapsed, bringing down a shower of sooty rainwater.

After about four hours of buffeting, the roof could take it no longer. My bedroom faces east, so my portion of the roof was the first to go.

The wind got under it and kept pushing until, with a ripping, groaning sound, the metal sheets shifted and slid off the rafters, some of them dropping with claps like thunder on the road below.

So that's it, I thought. Nothing worse can happen. As long as the ceiling stays on, I'm not getting out of bed. We'll collect our roof in the morning.

Icy water splashing down on my face made me change my mind in a hurry. Leaping from the bed, I found that much of the ceiling had gone, too. Water was pouring on my open typewriter as well as on the bedside radio and bed cover.

Picking up my precious typewriter (my companion for forty years) I stumbled into the front sitting room (and library), only to find a similar situation there. Water was pouring through the slats of the wooden ceiling, raining down on the open bookshelves.

By now I had been joined by the children, who had come to my rescue. Their section of the roof hadn't gone as yet. Their parents were struggling to close a window against the driving rain.

'Save the books!' shouted Dolly, the youngest, and that became our rallying cry for the next hour or two.

Dolly and her brother Mukesh picked up armfuls of books and carried them into their room. But the floor was awash, so the books had to be piled on their beds. Dolly was helping me gather some of my papers when a large field rat jumped onto the desk in front of her. Dolly squealed and ran for the door.

'It's all right,' said Mukesh, whose love of animals extends even to field rats. 'It's only sheltering from the storm.'

Big brother Rakesh whistled for our dog, Tony, but Tony wasn't interested in rats just then. He had taken shelter in the kitchen, the only dry spot in the house.

Two rooms were now practically roofless, and we could see the sky lit up by flashes of lightning.

There were fireworks indoors, too, as water spluttered and crackled along a damaged wire. Then the lights went out altogether.

Rakesh, at his best in an emergency, had already lit two kerosene lamps. And by their light we continued to transfer books, papers, and clothes to the children's room.

We noticed that the water on the floor was beginning to subside a little.

'Where is it going?' asked Dolly.

'Through the floor,' said Mukesh. 'Down to the flat below!'

Cries of concern from our downstairs neighbours told us that they were having their share of the flood.

Our feet were freezing because there hadn't been time to put on proper footwear. And besides, shoes and slippers were awash by now. All chairs and tables were piled high with books. I hadn't realised the extent of my library until that night!

The available beds were pushed into the driest corner of the children's room, and there, huddled in blankets and quilts, we spent the remaining hours of the night while the storm continued.

Towards morning the wind fell, and it began to snow. Through the door to the sitting room I could see snowflakes drifting through the gaps in the ceiling, settling on picture-frames. Ordinary things like a glue bottle and a small clock took on a certain beauty when covered with soft snow.

Most of us dozed off.

When dawn came, we found the windowpanes encrusted with snow and icicles. The rising sun struck through the gaps in the ceiling and turned everything golden. Snow crystals glistened on the empty bookshelves. But the books had been saved.

Rakesh went out to find a carpenter and tinsmith, while the rest of us started putting things in the sun to dry.

By evening we'd put much

of the roof back on.

It's a much-improved roof now, and we look forward to the next storm with confidence!

And Now We are Twelve

People often ask me why I've chosen to live in Mussoorie for so long – almost forty years, without any significant breaks.

'I forgot to go away,' I tell them, but of course, that isn't the real reason.

The people here are friendly, but then people are friendly in a great many other places. The hills, the valleys are beautiful; but they are just as beautiful in Kulu or Kumaon.

'This is where the family has grown up and where we all live,' I say, and those who don't know me are puzzled because the general impression of the writer is of a reclusive old bachelor.

Unmarried I may be, but single I am not. Not since Prem came to live and work with me in 1970. A year later, he was married.

Then his children came along and stole my heart; and when they grew up, their children came along and stole my wits. So now I'm an enchanted bachelor, head of a family of twelve. Sometimes I go out to bat, sometimes to bowl, but generally I prefer to be the twelfth man, carrying out the drinks.

In the old days, when I was a solitary writer living on baked beans, the prospect of my suffering from obesity was very remote. Now there is a little more of author than there used to be, and the other day five-year old Gautam patted me on my tummy (or balcony, as I prefer to call it) and remarked; 'Dada, you should join the WWF.'

'I'm already a member,' I said, 'I joined the World Wildlife Fund years ago.'

'Not that,' he said. 'I mean the World Wrestling Federation.'

If I have a tummy today, it's thanks to Gautam's grandfather and now his mother who, over the years, have made sure that I am well-fed and well-proportioned.

Forty years ago, when I was a lean young man, people would look at me and say, 'Poor chap, he's definitely undernourished. What on earth made him take up writing as a profession?' Now they look at me and say, 'You wouldn't think he was a writer, would you? Too well nourished!'

It was a cold, wet and windy March evening when Prem came back from the village with his wife and first-born child, then just four months old. In those days, they had to walk to the house from the bus stand; it was a half-hour walk in the cold rain, and the baby was all wrapped up when they entered the front room.

Finally, I got a glimpse of him. And he of me, and it was friendship at first sight. Little Rakesh (as he was to be called) grabbed me by the nose and held on. He did not have much of a nose to grab, but he had a dimpled chin and I played with it until he smiled.

The little chap spent a good deal of his time with me during those first two years in Maplewood – learning to crawl, to toddle, and then to walk unsteadily about the little sitting-room.

I would carry him into the garden, and later, up the steep gravel path to the main road.

Rakesh enjoyed these little excursions, and so did I, because in pointing out trees, flowers, birds, butterflies, beetles, grasshoppers, et al, I was giving myself a chance to observe them better instead of just taking them for granted.

In particular, there was a pair of squirrels that lived in the big oak tree outside the cottage. Squirrels are rare in Mussoorie though common enough down in the valley. This couple must have come up for the summer. They became quite friendly, and although they never got around to taking food from our hands, they were soon entering the house quite freely.

The sitting room window opened directly on to the oak tree whose various denizens – ranging from stag-beetles to small birds and even an acrobatic bat – took to darting in and out of the cottage at various times of the day or night.

Life at Maplewood was quite idyllic, and when Rakesh's baby brother, Suresh, came into the world, it seemed we were all set for a long period of domestic bliss; but at such times tragedy is often lurking just around the corner. Suresh was just over a year old when he contracted tetanus. Doctors and hospitals were of no avail.

He suffered – as any child would from this terrible affliction – and left this world before he had a chance of getting to know it. His parents were broken-hearted. And I feared for Rakesh, for he wasn't a very healthy boy, and two of his cousins in the village had already succumbed to tuberculosis.

It was to be a difficult year for me. A criminal charge was brought against me for a slightly risqué story I'd written for a Bombay magazine.

I had to face a trial in Bombay and this involved three journeys there over a period of a year and a half, before an irate but perceptive judge found the charges baseless and gave me an honourable acquittal.

It's the only time I've been involved with the law and I sincerely hope it is the last. Most cases drag on interminably, and the primary beneficiaries are the lawyers. My trial would have been much longer had not the prosecutor died of a heart attack in the middle of the proceedings. His successor did not pursue it with the same vigour. His heart was not in it.

The whole issue had started with a complaint by a local politician, and when he lost interest so did the prosecution. Nevertheless the trial, once begun, had to be seen through. The defence (organised by the concerned magazine) marshalled its witnesses (which included Nissim Ezekiel and the Marathi playwright Vijay Tendulkar).

I made a short speech which couldn't have been very memorable as I had forgotten it! And everyone, including the judge, was bored with the whole business. After that, I steered clear of controversial

publications.

I have never set out to shock the world. Telling a meaningful story was all that really mattered. And that is still the case.

I was looking forward to continuing our idyllic existence in Maplewood, but it was not to be. The powers-that-be, in the shape of the Public Works Department (PWD), had decided to build a 'strategic' road just below the cottage and without any warning to us, all the trees in the vicinity were felled (including the friendly old oak) and the hillside was rocked by explosives and bludgeoned by bulldozers. I decided it was time to move.

Prem and Chandra (Rakesh's mother) wanted to move too; not because of the road, but because they associated the house with the death of little Suresh, whose presence seemed to haunt every room, every corner of the cottage. His little cries of pain and suffering still echoed through the still hours of the night.

I rented rooms at the top of Landour, a good thousand feet higher up the mountain. Rakesh was now old enough to go to school, and every morning I would walk with him down to the little convent school near the clock tower.

Prem would go to fetch him in the afternoon. The walk took us about half-an-hour, and on the way Rakesh would ask for a story and I would have to rack my brains in order to invent one. I am not the most inventive of writers, and fantastical plots are beyond me.

My forte is observation, recollection, and reflection. Small boys prefer action. So I invented a leopard who suffered from acute indigestion because he'd eaten one human too many and a belt buckle was causing an obstruction.

This went down quite well until Rakesh asked me how the leopard got around the problem of the victim's clothes.

'The secret,' I said, 'is to pounce on them when their trousers are off!'

Not the stuff of which great picture books are made, but then, I've never attempted to write stories for beginners. Red Riding Hood's granny-eating wolf always scared me as a small boy, and yet parents have always found it acceptable for toddlers. Possibly they feel grannies are expendable.

Mukesh was born around this time and Savitri (Dolly) a couple of years later. When Dolly grew older, she was annoyed at having been named Savitri (my choice), which is now considered very old-fashioned; so we settled for Dolly. I can understand a child's dissatisfaction with given names.

My first name was Owen, which in Welsh means 'brave'. As I am not in the least brave, I have preferred not to use it. One given name and one surname should be enough.

When my granny said, 'But you should try to be brave, otherwise how will you survive in this cruel world?' I replied: 'Don't worry, I can run very fast.'

Not that I've ever had to do much running, except when I was pursued by a lissome Australian lady who thought I'd make a good obedient husband.

It wasn't so much the lady I was running from, but the prospect of spending the rest of my life in some remote cattle station in the Australian outback. Anyone who has

tried to drag me away from India has always met with stout resistance.

Up on the heights of Landour lived a motley crowd. My immediate neighbours included a Frenchwoman who played the sitar (very badly) all through the night; and a Spanish lady with two husbands, one of whom practised acupuncture – rather ineffectively as far as he was concerned, for he seemed to be dying of some mysterious debilitating disease.

Another neighbour came and went rather mysteriously, and finally ended up in Tihar jail, having been apprehended in Delhi carrying a large amount of contraband hashish.

Apart from these and a few other colourful characters, the area was inhabited by some very respectable people, retired brigadiers, air marshals and rear admirals, almost all of whom were busy writing their memoirs. I had to read or listen to extracts from their literary efforts.

This was slow torture. A few years before, I had done a stint of editing for a magazine called Imprint. It had involved going through hundreds of badly written

manuscripts, and in some cases (friends of the owner!) rewriting some of them for publication.

One of life's joys had been to throw up that particular job, and now here I was, besieged by all the top brass of the army, navy and air force, each one determined that I should read, inwardly digest, improve, and if possible find a publisher for their outpourings.

Thank goodness they were all retired. I could not be shot or court-martialled. But at least two of them set their wives upon me, and these intrepid ladies would turn up around noon with my 'homework' – typescripts to read and edit! There was no escape.

My own writing was of no consequence to them. I told them that I was taking sitar lessons, but they disapproved, saying I was more suited to the tabla.

When Prem discovered a set of vacant rooms further down the Landour slope, close to school and bazaar, I rented them without hesitation.

This was Ivy Cottage. Come up and see me sometime, but leave your manuscripts behind.

When we came to Ivy Cottage in 1980, we were six, Dolly has just been born. Now, twenty-four years later, we are twelve. I think that's a reasonable expansion.

The increase has been brought about by Rakesh's marriage twelve years ago, and Mukesh's marriage two years ago.

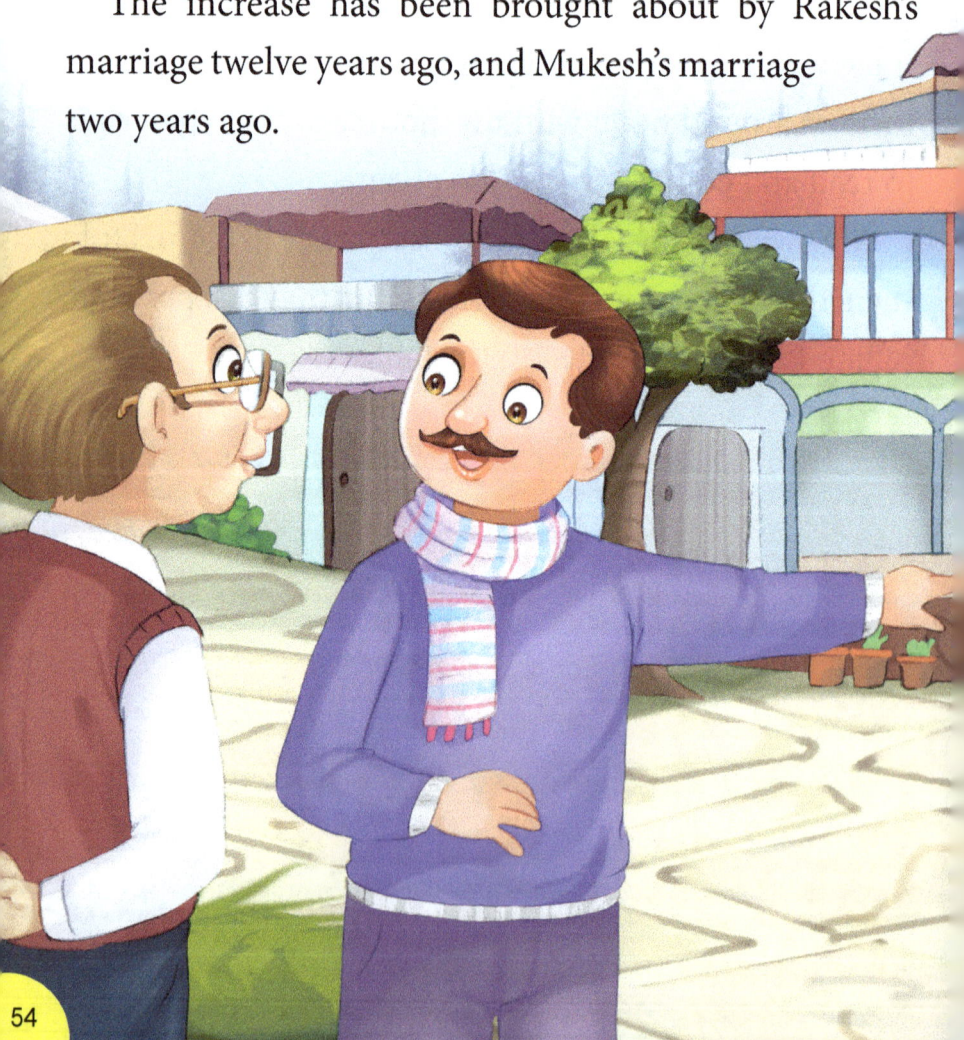

Both precipitated themselves into marriage when they were barely twenty, and both were lucky.

Beena and Binita, who happen to be real sisters, have brightened and enlivened our lives with their happy, positive natures and the wonderful children they have brought into the world. More about them later.

Ivy Cottage has, on the whole, been kind to us, and particularly kind to me. Some houses like their occupants, others don't. Maplewood, set in the shadow of the hill, lacked a natural cheerfulness; there was a settled gloom about the place. The house at the top of Landour was too exposed to the elements to have any sort of character.

The wind moaning in the deodars may have inspired the sitar player but it did nothing for my writing. I produced very little up there.

On the other hand, Ivy Cottage – especially my little room facing the sunrise – has been conducive to creative work. Novellas, poems, essays, children's stories, anthologies, have all come tumbling onto whatever sheets of paper happen to be nearest to me.

As I write by hand, I have only to grab for the nearest pad, loose sheet, page-proof or envelope whenever the muse takes hold of me; which is surprisingly often.

I came here when I was nearing fifty. Now I'm approaching eighty, and instead of drying up, as some writers do in their later years, I find myself writing with as much ease and assurance as when I was twenty. And I enjoy writing, it's not a burdensome task.

I may not have anything of earth-shattering significance to convey to the world, but in conveying my sentiments to you, dear readers, and in telling you something about my relationship with people and the natural world, I hope to bring a little pleasure and

sunshine into your life.

Life isn't a bed of roses, not for any of us, and I have never had the comforts or luxuries that wealth can provide. But here I am, doing my own thing, in my own time and my own way. What more can I ask of life?

Give me a big cash prize and I'd still be here. I happen to like the view from my window. And I like to have Gautam coming up to me, patting me on the tummy, and telling me that I'll make a good goalkeeper one day.

It's a Sunday morning, as I come to the conclusion of this chapter. There's bedlam in the house. Siddharth's football keeps smashing against the front door.

Shrishti is practising her dance routine in the back verandah. Gautam has cut his finger and is trying his best to bandage it with a cellotape.

He is, of course, the youngest of Rakesh's three musketeers, and probably the most independent-minded. Siddharth, now ten, is restless, never quite able to expend all his energy.

'Does not pay enough attention,' says his teacher.

It must be hard for anyone to pay attention in a class of sixty! How does the poor teacher pay attention?

If you, dear reader, have any ambitions to be a writer,

you must first rid yourself of any notion that perfect peace and quiet is the first requirement. There is no such thing as perfect peace and quiet except perhaps in a monastery or a cave in the mountains.

And what would you write about, living in a cave?

One should be able to write in a train, a bus, a bullock-cart, in good weather or bad, on a park bench or in the middle of a noisy classroom.

Of course, the best place is the sun-drenched desk right next to my bed. It isn't always sunny here, but on a good day like this, it's ideal. The children are getting ready for school, dogs are barking in the street, and down near the water tap there's an altercation between two women with empty buckets, the tap having dried up. But these are all background noises and will subside in due course. They are not directed at me.

Hello! Here's Atish, Mukesh's little ten-month old infant, crawling over the rug, curious to know why I'm sitting on the edge of my bed scribbling away, when I should be playing with him. So I shall play with him for five minutes and then come back to this page.

Giving him my time is essential. After all, I won't be around when he grows up.

Half-an-hour later, Atish was tired of playing with me, meanwhile Gautam had absconded with my pen. When I asked him to return it, he asked, 'Why don't you get a computer? Then we can play games on it.'

'My pen is faster than any computer,' I tell him. 'I wrote three pages this morning without getting out of bed. And yesterday I wrote two pages sitting under the chestnut tree.'

'Until a chestnut fell on your head,' says Gautam, 'did it hurt?'

'Only a little,' I said, putting on a brave front.

He had saved the chestnut and now he showed it to me. The smooth brown horse-chestnut shone in the sunlight.

'Let's stick it in the ground,' I said. 'Then in the spring a chestnut tree will come up.'

So we went outside and planted the chestnut on a plot of wasteland. Hopefully a small tree will burst through the earth at about the time this book is published.

Thirty years ago, Rakesh and I had planted a cherry seed on the hillside. It grew into a tree, which is still bursting with blossoms every year. Now it's Gautam's turn. And so we move on.